This book belongs to
_____

The Adventures of

Bella & Harry

Let's Visit Cairo!

Written By
Lisa Manzione

Illustrated By
Kristine Lucco

Bella & Harry, LLC

www.BellaAndHarry.com
email: BellaAndHarryGo@aol.com

Just as the sun began to rise, Harry looked out the window of his old palace hotel room.

"Bella! Wake up! I see huge triangles built on top of the ground."

5

"**Harry,** those triangles are the famous Pyramids of Giza."

"Pyramids of Giza? Where are we Bella?"

"Today, we are in Cairo, Egypt with our family. Egypt has a long history, dating back thousands of years."

6

"**The** pyramids you see are over 4,500 years old. The pyramids were built of limestone and granite and are about 64–65 camels tall... or about 450 feet in height!"

"Harry, let's get a closer look at the pyramids."

7

"Look! Our children are riding a camel near the pyramids!
Let's ride with them!"

"Bella, I heard that camels store water in their humps.
Is that really true?"

"**No** Harry, that is not true. Camels store fat in their humps. The fat is used for energy during times when the camel does not have any food to eat. Camels can go for several months without eating food while traveling through the desert."

"Ohhhh! That is a really long time without a snack!"

9

"Harry, if you look over there, you will see the Great Sphinx. The Sphinx was most likely carved out of bedrock, with the support of limestone... really, really hard rocks. The Sphinx is one of the oldest, largest surviving sculptures of the ancient world."

"WOW! How cool, Bella! Do you think
we can take a closer look at the Sphinx?"

"Sure, Harry. Let's go!"

"Look at the face, Harry. It looks like the face of a person, with the body of a lion. No one knows for sure, but most historians believe this is a tribute to a pharaoh who ruled during the fourth dynasty... or in puppy terms, a very, very, very long time ago!"

"Bella, I want to be pharaoh!"

"Okay, Harry! Maybe one day you will be pharaoh! Right now, we are two young pups learning about this fascinating country called Egypt."

13

"Let's go, Harry! We are traveling by minivan through the city. Next stop... The Museum of Egyptian Antiquities! We are going to see mummies!"

"Mummies?

Bella, I thought our mummy was in the car with us?"

"Oh Harry, you are very funny! I am not talking about our mommy! I am talking about 'mummies'! When people in Egypt passed away thousands of years ago, they were prepared for burial in a special way called mummification. After that, they were called mummies."

ANCIENT EGYPT

MUMMIES

"**Harry!** Look at all of the history in this museum! Have you ever heard of King Tutankhamun?"

"No, Bella. I have never heard of King Tutankhamun. Who was he?"

"King Tutankhamun, or King Tut, was a very famous boy king. It is believed that he became king at the age of 8 or 9 years old. He only ruled for about 10 years. When his tomb was found in 1922, it was filled with gold and treasures. See the mask, Harry? It is made of gold with jewels and colored glass paste!"

"Off we go Harry. We are headed to the 'Royal Mummy Room'."

18

"Bella, it is very cold in this room. Burrrh....."

"Yes, the room has to be kept at 70 degrees fahrenheit. These mummies were the Royalty of ancient Egypt. The mummies are thousands of years old!"

"**Harry,** it is time for our road trip! We are heading to the Valley of the Kings, just outside of Luxor, Egypt. While we are in the minivan, let's look at the map together. The pyramid shows the location of Cairo and the statue shows the location of Luxor."

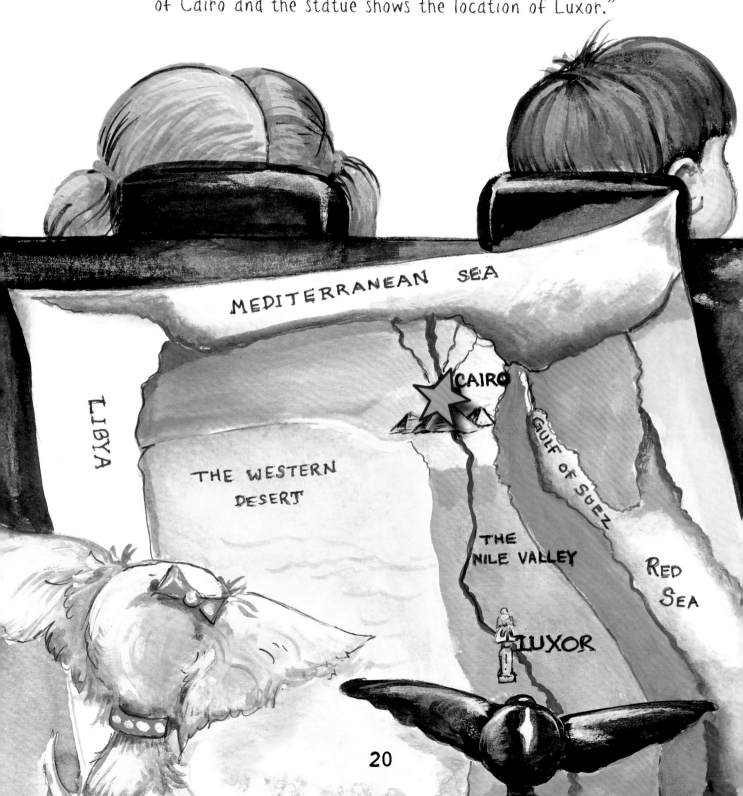

MEDITERRANEAN SEA

LIBYA

CAIRO

THE WESTERN DESERT

GULF OF SUEZ

THE NILE VALLEY

RED SEA

LUXOR

"**Look** to your right, Harry. The statues you see are the Colossi of Memnon. The statues have stood for over 3,400 years!"

"Next stop... Valley of the Kings! The Valley of the Kings is one of the most visited places in Egypt!"

"Currently, there are 63 discovered tombs located here in the Valley of the Kings. Several other areas near the Valley of the Kings, such as the Valley of the Queens, have tombs as well. All of the tombs are built underground. Harry, we will take the stairs down into the tomb."

"Be sure to look at all of the wonderful drawings and paintings on the wall, Harry. They are actually letters that look like pictures and are called hieroglyphics. The ancient Egyptians used hieroglyphics to write names and messages."

TOMB
OF
RAMESSES IIII

"Ohhhh... Bella! The paintings are so colorful!
Do you think we can learn to paint?"

"Yes Harry, I think we can learn to paint when we get home. Right
now we are heading back to Cairo. Let's go!"

24

"Bella, look over there! I see a statue of feet!"

"**Well,** Harry, that is the Ramesseum. Ramesses II, or 'Ramesses the Great', ruled for about 67 years. Many large buildings and temples, including the Ramesseum, were built while Ramesses was the ruler of Egypt."

27

"Look at the statue on the ground Harry. See the hieroglyphics on the shoulder of the statue? It was a very common practice of the stone carvers to include the name of the ruler on the statue."

"I have a great idea! When we return to our hotel room, let's see if we can spell our names in hieroglyphics."

"Oh, Bella! We can't do that. We never learned to write in hieroglyphics!"

"You are right, Harry! How silly! Let's go for a felucca ride instead!"

"Bella, what is a felucca?"

"A felucca is very similar to a sail boat. The feluccas are powered by the wind and usually seat about 8 – 12 passengers. Feluccas have been sailing the Nile River for thousands of years."

"Is the Nile River a big river, Bella?"

"Yes Harry, the Nile River is the longest river in the world. Keep your eyes open for Nile crocodiles!"

30

"Whew! That was a lot of fun! Now, it's time for dinner. It looks like grilled vegetables with rice is being served, along with figs for dessert. Fresh vegetables and fruit are served often in Egypt."

31

Well, we hope you enjoyed the tour of Egypt with us!
We can't wait for our next adventure with you!
We really would love to have you join us!

For now... it's good-bye, or "ma'as salama" in Arabic,
from Bella Boo and Harry too!

32

Our Adventure to Cairo

Having fun near the Step Pyramid.

Kissing the Sphinx.

Harry looking at a copy of the Nefertiti Bust. The original bust is in a German museum.

Posing with Bastet, an ancient goddess.

Harry and Anubis.

Harry sitting in King Tut's chair.

Exploring the Avenue of the
Sphinxes in Luxor, Egypt.

Bella & Harry visiting the
Solar Boat Museum.

Hieroglyphic Alphabet

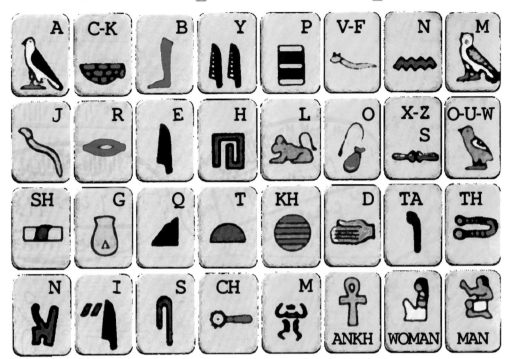

A	C-K	B	Y	P	V-F	N	M
J	R	E	H	L	O	X-Z S	O-U-W
SH	G	Q	T	KH	D	TA	TH
N	I	S	CH	M	ANKH	WOMAN	MAN

Spell your name in Hieroglyphics

Library of Congress Cataloging-in-Publications Data is available

Manzione, Lisa

The Adventures of Bella & Harry: Let's Visit Cairo!

ISBN: 978-1-937616-04-5

First Edition

Book Four of Bella & Harry Series

For further information please visit:

www.BellaAndHarry.com

or

Email: BellaAndHarryGo@aol.com

CPSIA Section 103 (a) Compliant

www.beaconstar.com/ consumer

ID: L0118329. Tracking No.: L1412420

Printed in China